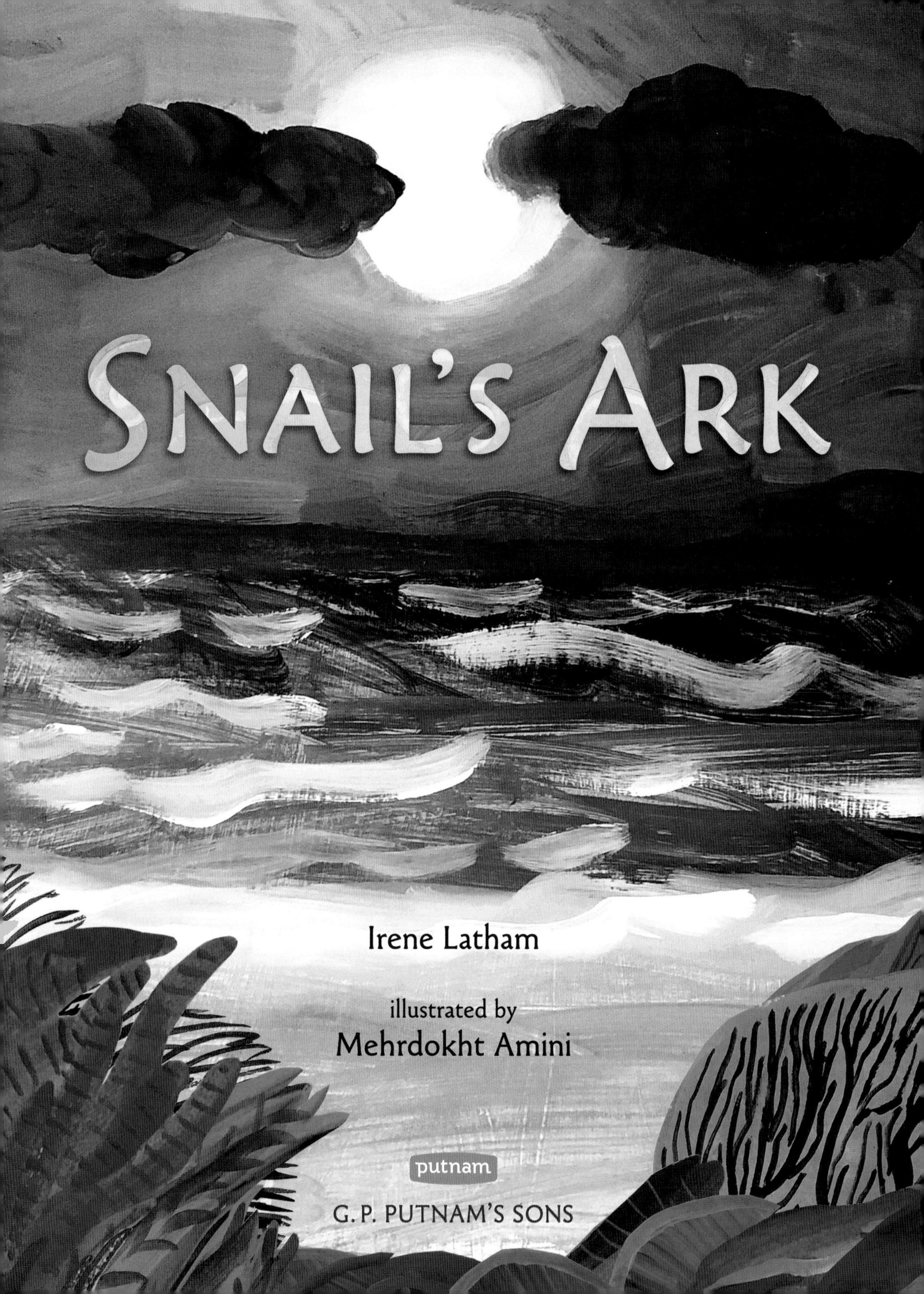

SNAIL'S ARK

Irene Latham

illustrated by
Mehrdokht Amini

putnam

G. P. PUTNAM'S SONS

For my PAH friends Amy, April,
Doraine, Jeannine, Linda & Robyn:
thank you, thank you. —I.L.

To all children, I hope you have
as fun a ride as our snails. —M.A.

Esther woke early.
Her antlers waved.
The air was sharp,
like before a storm.
Something was happening.
Something big.

The ground vibrated with footsteps—

heavy ones,
hooved ones,
clawed ones.

Hurry, hurry! the ground said.

Quickly, Esther sealed herself
into her shell and said a little prayer.

Please don't let me get crushed by an elephant!
Please don't let me get crushed by an elephant!

She didn't.

Her stomach squeezed
as she trailed toward a fallen
log ripe with golden mushrooms.
Above her, the sky hummed with wings—

feathered ones,
furred ones,
transparent ones.

Hurry, hurry! the sky said.

Esther was so overwhelmed, she crashed into a spiderweb. But it didn't matter. The spider was already gone.

Beside her, the river gurgled with swimmers—

slick ones,
scaly ones,
whiskered ones.

Hurry, hurry, the river said. *Before the rain starts.*

Rain? Esther didn't mind rain.
She was a snail. She could always snuggle
into a crack and nap through the storm.

Not this storm, the wind said.

Esther inched forward, her antlers
swaying wildly. Did her friend Solomon
know about the storm? She decided
to check the fern glade before moving
any closer to the giant *something*.

She climbed up a fern frond. It bent
into a gentle arc, tipping her onto
the ground—right in front of Solomon.

Hurry, hurry!
she told her friend
as raindrops began to fall—

cold ones,
quick ones,
splashy ones.

Esther led Solomon onto the smooth,
glossy surface of a newly fallen leaf.
She told him to press his sticky foot against
the leaf until it stuck like glue. Solomon did.

Please, Esther prayed. *Help us.*

And that's when it happened.
A brisk wind gusted against
her shell, and the whole world
began to whirl.

The wind lifted the two snails up and up
until they were sailing across the sky.
They were flying!

When the snails landed,
their antlers detected
many strange animals—

excited ones,
frightened ones,
grateful ones.

Thank you,
thank you,
the snails said.

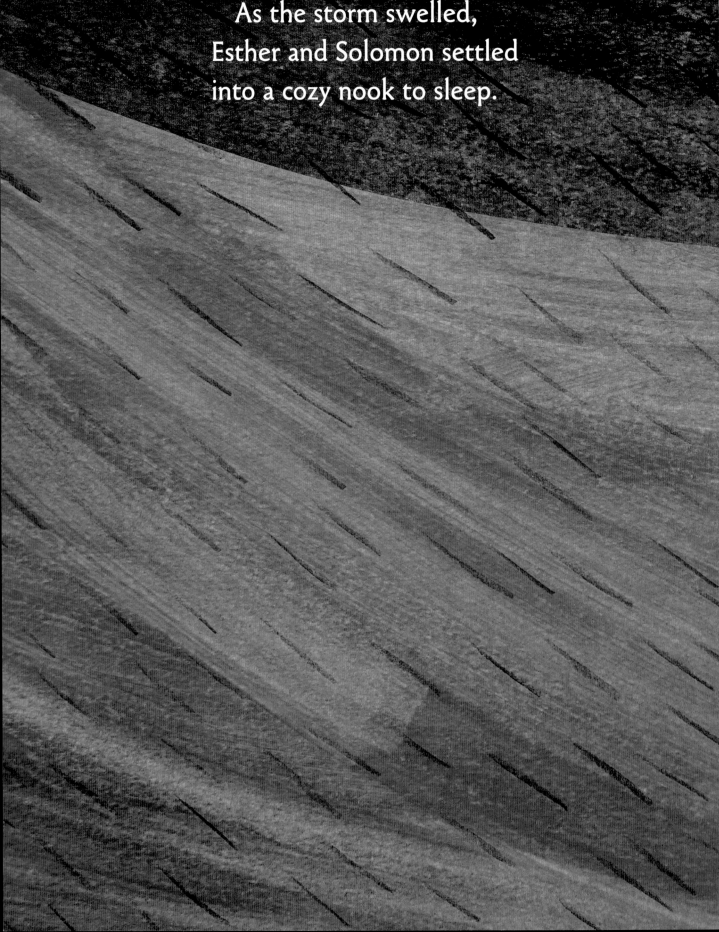

As the storm swelled,
Esther and Solomon settled
into a cozy nook to sleep.

G. P. PUTNAM'S SONS
An imprint of Penguin Random House LLC, New York

First published in the United States of America by G. P. Putnam's Sons,
an imprint of Penguin Random House LLC, 2022

Text copyright © 2022 by Irene Latham
Illustrations copyright © 2022 by Mehrdokht Amini

Visit us online at penguinrandomhouse.com

Library of Congress Cataloging-in-Publication Data is available.

Manufactured in Spain
ISBN 9780593109397
1 3 5 7 9 10 8 6 4 2
EST

Design by Nicole Rheingans
Text set in Paradigm Pro
The artwork was hand drawn mostly by acrylic-gouache
and then collaged in separate layers using Adobe Photoshop.